Best-Loved Paddington Stories

Paddington at the Circus

by Michael Bond

Paddington Goes to Hospital

by Michael Bond
& Karen Jankel

Paddington Goes for Gold

by Michael Bond

Illustrated by R. W. Alley

HarperCollins *Children's Books*

Action Medical Research and Paddington Bear

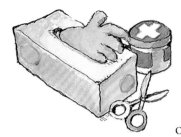

Paddington Bear has been at the heart of fundraising for Action Medical Research ever since his creator, Michael Bond, met the charity's founder, Duncan Guthrie, in 1976.

Paddington's cheery face has helped Action Medical Research attract thousands of new supporters, raising millions of pounds to treat sick babies and children in the UK and can often be found at fundraising events up and down the country.

Since 1952, Action Medical Research has spent more than £115 million on research that has helped save thousands of lives and changed many more. Its earliest research contributed to the development and rapid adoption of the first UK polio vaccines. Since then, it has supported further breakthroughs in medical care, including vaccines for rubella and Hib meningitis, the use of ultrasound scanning in pregnancy and awareness of the importance of taking folic acid during pregnancy to prevent spina bifida.

But there is still so much more to do. Paddington would love you to find out more about his favourite UK charity and how you can help, by visiting www.action.org.uk

This edition first published in paperback in Great Britain by HarperCollins *Children's Books* in 2017

Paddington at the Circus first published in hardback by HarperCollins*Publishers*, USA, in 2000
First published in hardback in Great Britain by Collins Picture Books in 2000
First published in paperback by Collins in 2001
Revised edition published by HarperCollins *Children's Books* in 2016

Paddington Goes to Hospital first published in hardback in Great Britain by HarperCollins*Publishers* Ltd in 2001
First published in paperback by Collins Picture Books in 2002
New edition published by HarperCollins *Children's Books* in 2012
Revised edition published in 2015

Paddington Goes for Gold first published in hardback in Great Britain by HarperCollins *Children's Books* in 2012
First published in paperback in 2012
Revised edition published in 2015

9 10

ISBN: 978-0-00-824503-0

Collins Picture Books is an imprint of HarperCollins*Publishers* Ltd.
HarperCollins *Children's Books* is a division of HarperCollins*Publishers* Ltd
1 London Bridge Street, London SE1 9GF

www.harpercollins.co.uk

HarperCollins*Publishers*, 1st Floor, Watermarque Building, Ringsend Road, Dublin 4, Ireland

Paddington at the Circus and *Paddington Goes for Gold*: Text copyright © Michael Bond 2000, 2012
Paddington Goes to Hospital: Text copyright © Michael Bond and Karen Jankel 2001
Illustrations copyright © R. W. Alley 2000, 2001, 2011, 2012

Printed in Italy

Paddington

at the Circus

One morning Paddington was doing his shopping in the market when he saw a very tall man with a pointed hat and baggy trousers.

The man was putting up a poster, and he was so tall, he didn't even need a ladder to reach the top of the billboard.

The poster showed a huge tent decorated with coloured lights, and across the middle were the words SEE THE WORLD'S GREATEST CIRCUS! ONE NIGHT ONLY.

Paddington rubbed his eyes several times in order to make sure he wasn't dreaming.

Paddington hurried back home to tell the others what he had seen.

"The world's greatest circus?" repeated Jonathan, giving his sister a wink. "Are you sure?"

"It's for one night only!" exclaimed Paddington.

"Don't worry," said Judy. "You won't miss it."

"Dad's got tickets for the front row," added Jonathan. "Mrs Bird's coming, too."

Paddington had never been to a circus before, and he was very excited at the thought. "I hope it gets dark early," he said. "Then we can see the lights."

Paddington's wish came true. Seen from the outside,
with all the coloured lights twinkling against the night
sky, the circus really did have a magical air.

"Hurry! Hurry! Have your tickets ready!" called
a voice. "The show's about to begin."

"It's the man I saw this morning," whispered
Paddington. "The very tall one I was telling you about."

"That's one of the clowns," said Judy.

"He isn't really that tall…" began Jonathan.
But Paddington couldn't wait. He could hear a
band playing, and he was already hurrying on ahead.

But if the outside of the tent had seemed exciting, it was nothing compared to the inside.

There was a lovely smell of sawdust, and in amongst the jugglers and the acrobats there was even a girl selling ice cream.

Mr Brown pointed to a man in the middle of the ring. He was wearing a top hat.

"That's the ringmaster," he explained. "He's in charge of everything."

"I expect you could keep a lot of marmalade sandwiches under a hat like that," said Paddington enviously. "I think I would like to be a ringmaster one day."

Just then the tall clown entered the ring. He was clutching a long pole that had a bucket balanced on the end of it. When he saw Paddington waving, he came across to greet him.

"Watch out!" cried Jonathan, as the clown leaned over to shake Paddington's paw.

Paddington jumped up in alarm. But he wasn't quick enough. Before he had time to escape, the bucket had fallen off the end of the pole.

Luckily, it was tied on
with string and it was
empty, so Paddington
didn't get wet.

"Clowns are full of tricks,"
said Judy.

"I'm glad I was wearing my
duffle coat all the same,"
said Paddington.

"Someone might have
put water in the bucket
by mistake."

"I'm told ice cream is very good for young bears if they've had a shock," said Mr Brown.

He ordered six large cones, then they all sat back to enjoy the show.

"I feel better already, Mr Brown," said Paddington gratefully.

Paddington had hardly started on his ice
cream when he had yet another shock.
Glancing up towards the roof of the tent,
he saw a man hanging from a rope.
Jonathan looked at his programme.
"That must be one of the Popular Prices,"
he said. "They're trapeze artists."
"Don't worry!" called Paddington.
"I'm coming. Bears are good at climbing."

Before the others could stop him, Paddington was halfway up the nearest tent pole.

Climbing the pole and carrying an ice cream at the same time wasn't easy, and the audience gave a round of applause when he reached the safety of a small platform near the top.

Paddington was about to take a bow, when to his surprise he saw a man coming towards him on a bicycle.

"I don't think you're supposed to bring your bicycle up here, Mr Price!" he exclaimed.

"Look out!" shouted the man,
frantically ringing his bell. "I can't stop!"
"Hold on!" called his partner.

In the confusion, Paddington didn't know which to do first,
so he grabbed hold of a nearby bar.

It came away in his paw, and before he knew what
was happening, he felt himself flying through the air.

The audience thought Paddington was
part of the act, and they clapped
louder than ever.
Then a gasp went up as he missed
the platform on the other
side of the tent and began
swinging backwards
and forwards in midair.

"Oh, dear!" said Mrs Brown. "Whatever will he do now?"

"I shouldn't worry," said Mrs Bird. "Bears usually land on their feet."

But even Mrs Bird went quiet as Paddington's swings got slower and
slower, until finally he ended up hanging over the middle of the ring.

"Don't let go!" shouted the ringmaster. "Whatever you do – don't let go!"

"I'm not going to!" cried Paddington.

He tried to raise his hat, but he was still holding the ice cream cone in his other paw.

A look of horror came over the ringmaster's face as something soft and white landed with a squelch on his beautifully clean top hat.

"Help!" cried Paddington. "I've changed my mind. I can't hold on much longer."

Everybody in the audience began making suggestions, but in the end it was the clown who came to the rescue. Balancing his bucket on the end of the pole, he stretched up as high as he could so that Paddington could climb into it.

"I hope the string doesn't break," said Mrs Bird. "That bear had a very large lunch."

"If the clown stretches any more," said Judy, "his trousers will fall down."

Sure enough they did, and the cheers changed
to laughter as Paddington was lowered to safety.

"Funniest act I've seen in years!" shouted a man near the Browns. "More! More!"

Paddington gave the man a hard stare. "I don't think I want to do any more," he announced. "In fact, I don't think I want to go on a trapeze ever again. I shall just sit and watch from now on."

Then he caught sight of the clown's stilts. "It's no wonder you look so tall!" he exclaimed.

Paddington didn't think anything more *could* happen to him, but at the end of the evening the ringmaster presented him with another ice cream and insisted he take part in the Grand Parade.

"After all," he said, "you *were* the star of the show."

"It's a pity we are moving on," he added, turning to the Browns. "It isn't every evening we have a daring young bear on the flying trapeze."

"If you ask me," said Mrs Bird wisely, "it's a good thing you don't. Otherwise there's no knowing where you would end up."

Later that evening, when the Browns said good night to
Paddington, they found him standing on the box seat by his
bedroom window. He had a faraway look in his eyes.

"I was taking a last look at the circus before it goes on
its way," he explained.

"Do you still want to be a ringmaster
one day?" asked Judy.

Paddington lay back on the lawn with his paws in the air and gazed up at the Browns. "Where am I?" he gasped.

"You're at home, dear," said Mrs Brown. "At number thirty-two, Windsor Gardens."

"Is that in Darkest Peru?" asked Paddington.

"If you ask me," said Mrs Bird, "that bear's lost his memory."

"Oh dear, Henry!" exclaimed Mrs Brown. "What shall we do?"

Mr Brown consulted his Medical Dictionary. "All it says here is, 'the victim shouldn't drive a car'."

"I don't think I could anyway," said Paddington. "I've hurt my shoulder."

"Would you like a bun?" suggested Mrs Brown.

"What's a bun?" asked Paddington.

"That settles it," said Mrs Bird.
"I'm phoning the hospital!"

"I'm sorry we took so long," said the ambulance driver. "When I heard the name 'Paddington' I went to the railway station by mistake. If you ask me," he added, "this young bear's not only lost his memory, he's put his shoulder out as well. One of you ladies had better come with him in case he has to stay in hospital overnight."

"Thank goodness I put his clean pyjamas out this morning," said Mrs Bird, trying to strike a cheerful note.

The ambulance crew soon made up for lost time, and with sirens wailing, Paddington reached the hospital in no time at all.

"Stand by for a young bear emergency," said the driver to the waiting staff, and with a count of three, they lifted Paddington on to a bed.

"Is it true that you've lost your memory?" asked a doctor.

"Would you mind repeating the question?" replied Paddington. "Phew! Phew!"

"I don't like the sound of his wheezes," said a nurse.

"I've think we've got complications," agreed the doctor. "He'd better go straight to x-ray."

"You've got complications!" exclaimed Paddington indignantly. "What about me? Phew! Phew!"

Paddington had never travelled anywhere on a bed before and he thought it was very good value. "There was nothing like this in Darkest Peru," he announced as they gathered speed. "Phew! Phew!"

When they reached the x-ray room, the lady in charge pushed
a large machine over the bed and made some adjustments.

"Now lie very still while I take some pictures," she said.
"Otherwise, they will come out blurred."

With that she went to the other side of the room, pressed a
button, and there was a whirring noise.

"Cheese!" said Paddington.

Afterwards, Paddington and Mrs Brown met the doctor again.

Paddington stared at the pictures on the wall. "What's happened to my fur?" he exclaimed. "I had it when I came in."

"It's still there," said the doctor. "This is a special camera for looking inside people – and bears, too," he added hastily.

"It looks very complicated," said Paddington. "I didn't know I had so much inside me."

"The one on the left shows why your shoulder's hurting," explained the doctor. "The bone's come out of its socket. We shall need to put you to sleep while we relocate it."

"Have you had anything to eat since breakfast?" asked a nurse. "I haven't even had time for my elevenses," said Paddington.

"That's good," said the nurse, wiping his arm with something cold. "Otherwise you would have had to wait while it settled."

Paddington felt a tiny prick, and he was about to give the nurse a hard stare…

…when his eyelids began to go droopy.

As soon as he was asleep the doctor turned to Mrs Brown. "We'll soon put things right. He won't feel a thing.

"As for his memory, it probably needs a jog, but a good night's rest often works wonders. I must say I'm a bit worried about his breathing, though."

"It's a mystery," said Mrs Brown. "He's never had this problem before."

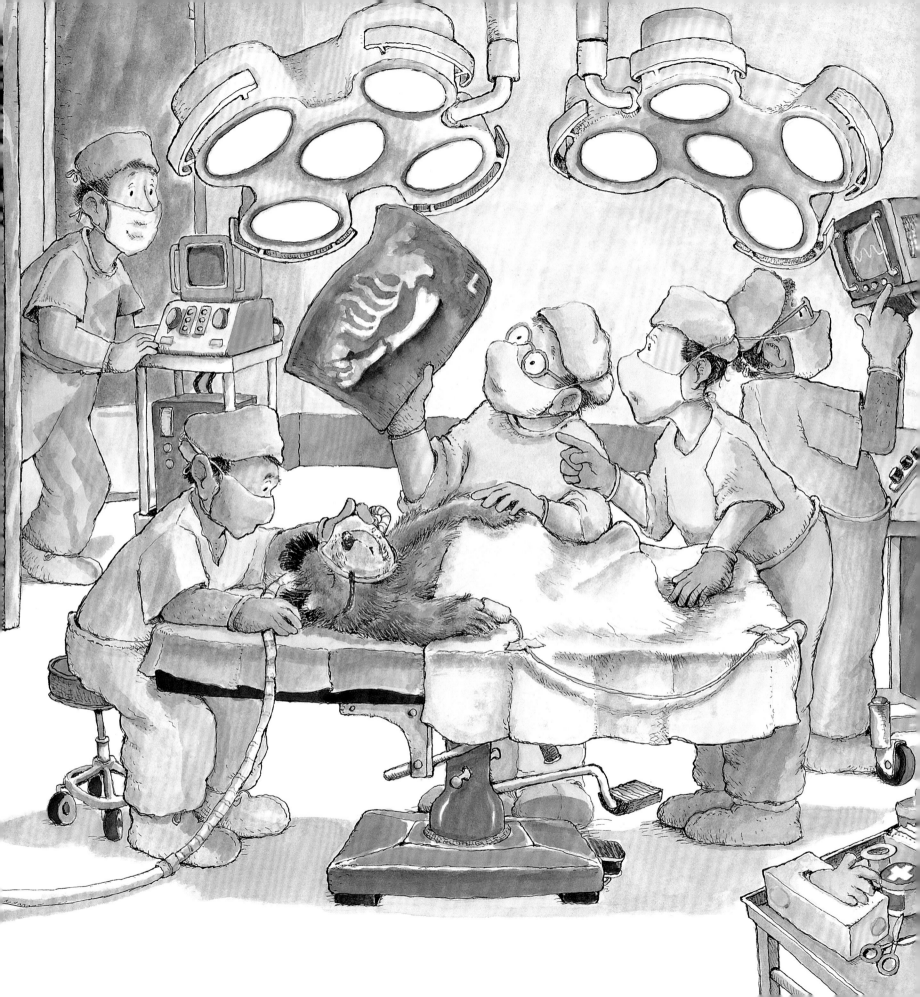

Paddington woke to find himself in a strange room.

"Where am I?" he asked for the second time that day.

"You're in a ward with lots of other patients," said Mrs Brown. "And the doctor's put your arm back in its socket."

"I hope it's pointing the right way," said Paddington. "Otherwise, I shan't know whether I'm coming or going."

"I've brought you some water," said a nurse. "I expect you're feeling thirsty after your operation."

"I am," said Paddington.

He was about to ask for something more exciting to drink, but he couldn't think of the name.

"Tea?" suggested Mrs Brown.

"Bless you!" said Paddington.

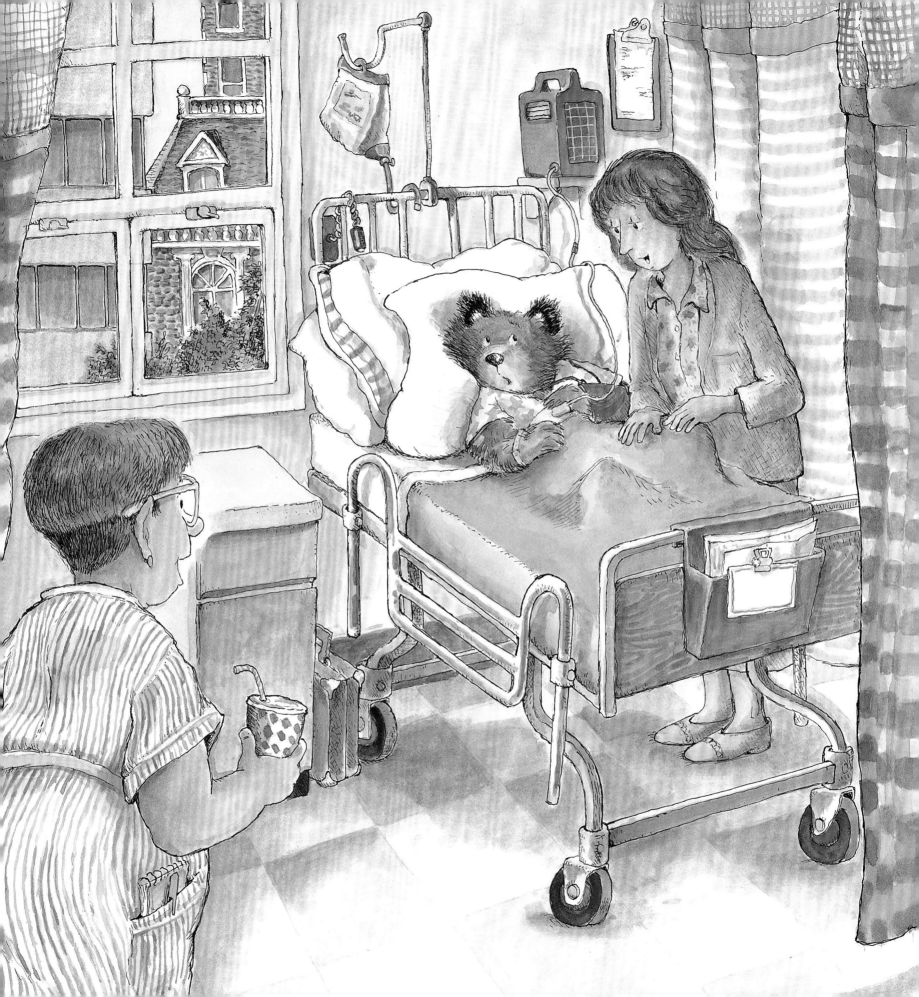

"I expect they will keep you in overnight for observation," said Mrs Brown.

"I don't think I want anyone observing me asleep," said Paddington. "I might fall out of bed."

"Don't worry," said the nurse. "The sides lift up to stop that happening."

"Besides, I shan't be far away," said Mrs Brown.

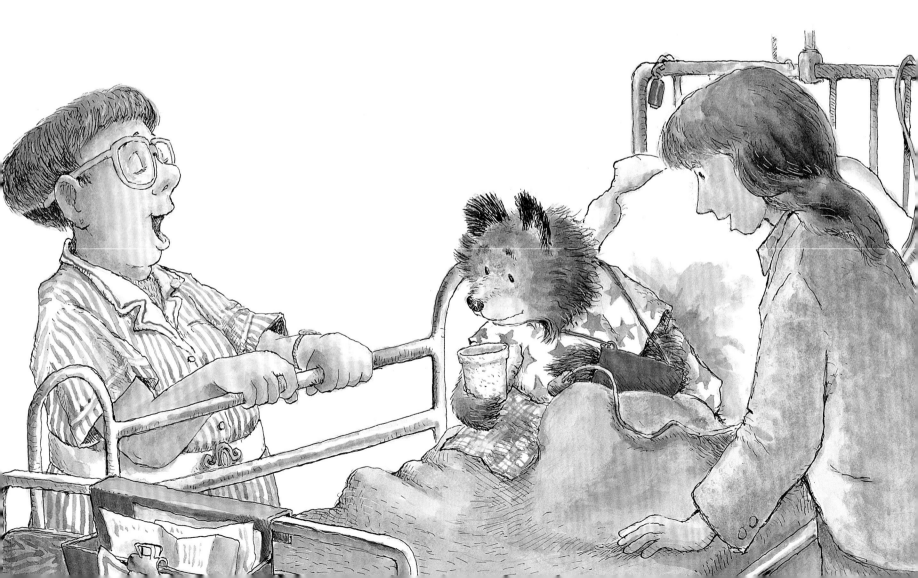

At that moment Mr Brown arrived, carrying a bowl of fruit from all the traders in the market and a 'Get Well Soon' card from Paddington's friend, Mr Gruber.

"Even Mr Curry sent his best wishes," he said. "What it is to be popular."

The lady who brought Paddington's supper had been surprised to see him. "The boy who used to be in your bed liked his food hot and spicy," she warned. "I hope it's suitable for bears."

Paddington had told her not to worry.

"There's nothing wrong with your appetite," said a nurse, eyeing the empty plate.

"There is now!" gasped Paddington. And this time his 'phews!' sounded as though he really meant them, for he had never before tasted anything quite so hot.

"I think I'd better leave taking your temperature until you've cooled down," said the nurse. "I'll simply feel your pulse to be going on with."

Just then two more nurses came along pushing a trolley laden with bottles and jars.

"It's medicine time," said one of them, handing Paddington a small cup filled with pink liquid.

"I'd like another one of those, please," he announced. "I think it's doing me good already."

The nurse laughed. "I wish we had more patients like you."

When it was bedtime, Mrs Brown helped Paddington wash his whiskers and clean his teeth.

"If you need anything in the night," she said, "just press the emergency button and someone will come."

"Sleep tight," she said, lifting the sides on the bed.

"Oh, I shall," murmured Paddington. So much had happened to him he felt as though he might sleep for ever.

"I think," he announced to the world in general, "I might have an emergency button by my bed when I get home. I often want things in the night."

But he didn't have time to test the one in the hospital, for he was soon fast asleep.

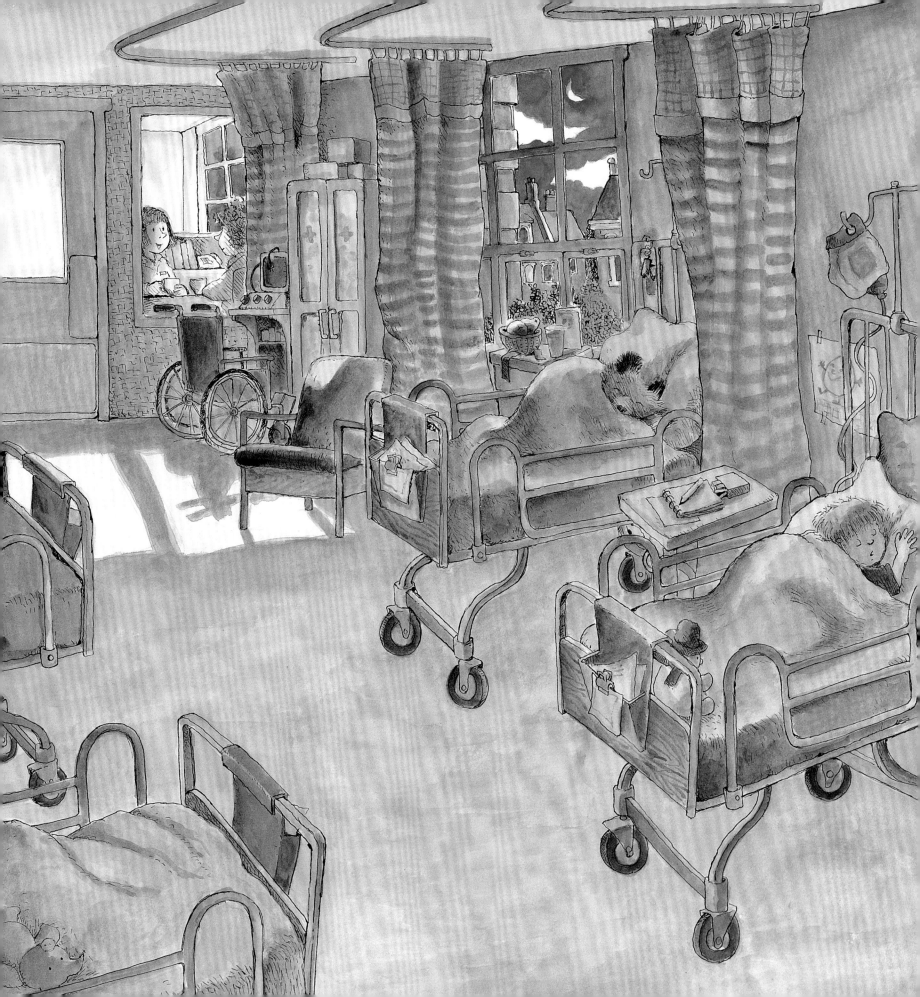

Next morning, Paddington went for a walk round
the ward to meet the other patients.

One small boy had just
had his tonsils removed.

Another had fallen out
of a tree and broken his leg.

A girl had been rushed in to
have her appendix out.

Another boy had been knocked down by a car when he
ran across the road without looking.

Paddington decided he was really very lucky.

"You can always see people worse
off than yourself in a hospital,"
said a nurse.

"I can see why they're called
patients," said Paddington.
"Some of them must have
to wait a very long
time before they
get better."

To Paddington's surprise, when he got back to
his bed he found he had visitors.

Mr Brown held up an L-shaped piece of wood. "Do you recognise this?" he asked. "I found it when I was cutting the grass this morning."

"It's my boomerang!" exclaimed Paddington. "The one you gave me for my birthday. It's all coming back to me."

"Like it did yesterday morning!" said Mrs Bird. "Blessed thing! It must have flown back when you were testing it and hit you on the head."

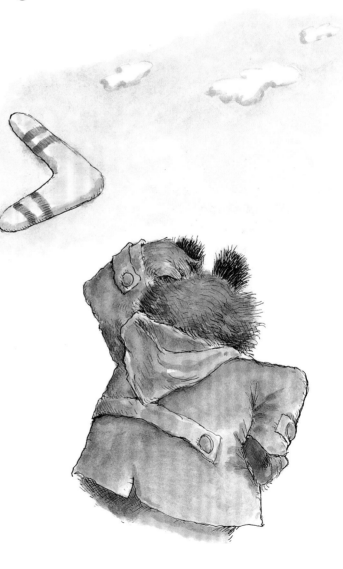

"That's the trouble with boomerangs," said Jonathan. "They always come back."

"You'd better duck next time," agreed Judy.

"It's all your fault, Henry," said
Mrs Brown. "No wonder
Paddington lost his memory."

"Well, at least it seems to have
been jogged back again," said
Mr Brown defensively.

"Phew! Phew!" agreed Paddington.

"And that's another thing," said
Mrs Bird. She held up a small silver
object. "Guess what?"

"It's the present you gave me in case I ever have an emergency,"
said Paddington. "It must have fallen out of my pocket." He held
the object up to his mouth and blew, "Phew! Phew!"

Several piercing blasts brought doctors and nurses running from
all directions.

"It's nice to know it isn't broken. When I lost my memory,
I forgot I needed a whistle to make my 'phews' work,"
said Paddington.

"All's well that ends well," said the doctor,
as the Browns explained what had happened.
"It's been a learning experience for us, too,"
he added, amid general agreement.
"It could come in very useful if we have any
more bear patients to look after."
"I'm glad you had me to practise on,"
said Paddington, as he waved goodbye.
"I've never been in a hospital before,
and now that I know what goes on,
I shall never mind
coming back!"

HOSP
QUI
PLEA

Paddington

Goes for Gold

One morning Paddington was lingering by the Browns' front door at number thirty-two Windsor Gardens in case a postcard arrived from his Aunt Lucy in Peru, when to his surprise a leaflet came through the letter box and landed on his nose.

Paddington didn't normally take much notice of leaflets, and he was about to throw it in the nearest waste bin when the words FREE ENTRY and PRIZES caught his eye. It sounded much more interesting than usual, so he decided to show the leaflet to Mr Brown when he came home from work that evening.

"It's from the local sports club," explained Mr Brown over dinner that evening. "They're holding a fund-raising event tomorrow. There's something for everyone, and prizes galore."

"There's even a knitting competition," announced Paddington, for Mrs Bird's benefit.

The Browns' housekeeper gave a non-committal grunt.

"Let's go, Dad," chorused Jonathan and Judy. "It sounds fun."

"Well…" began Mr Brown. "I was picturing a round of golf."

"I'll iron your shorts, Henry," said Mrs Brown. "They could do with an airing."

"If they still fit me," said Mr Brown gloomily.

The Browns set off in high spirits early the next day, but it was short-lived, for as they entered the sports ground the first person they bumped into was Mr Curry. Their next-door neighbour could put a damper on anything.

Worse still, he was making a beeline for Paddington.

"I suppose it had to happen," murmured Mr Brown. "That leaflet must have gone to all the houses in the area."

"Hold this ball for a moment, bear," boomed Mr Curry, thrusting a round object into Paddington's paws.

Mr Curry roared with laughter as Paddington staggered backwards.

"Caught you out for once, bear," he chuckled. "It's made of lead and it's used for what's called Putting the Shot. You're supposed to throw it as hard as you can."

Mrs Bird took a firm grip of her handbag, but she had no need of it, for Mr Curry suddenly gave a roar of pain.

"Bear!" he bellowed, hopping on one leg. "What do you think you're doing?"

"You said I was supposed to throw it," exclaimed Paddington. "I'm afraid it didn't go very far."

"Far enough to land on my foot. I don't forget things in a hurry!" cried Mr Curry.

"No prizes there, I'm afraid," called a steward, joining the group. "Anyone for the three-legged race? You'd better hurry. It's about to start."

Jonathan and Judy made a dash for it, closely followed by Paddington, only too anxious to escape Mr Curry's wrath.

"But you've got four legs between you," Paddington hissed. "Two and two makes four."

"Don't worry," Judy removed her ribbon. "If we tie two of them together that makes three."

"Leave it to me," said Paddington. "Bears are good at knots."

"Ready…" called the starter. "Steady… Go!"

Jonathan tore off straight away, but Judy was unable to move.

"Oh dear," said Paddington. "I think I must have tied the wrong two legs together by mistake."

"No prizes there either I'm afraid," said the steward. He turned to Mr Brown. "Shall I put you down for the hundred metre hurdles?"

"Actually," said Mr Brown, "I rather fancy the slow bicycle race. I used to be a dab hand at it when I was a boy."

"I'm for the knitting competition," said Mrs Bird. "I've brought my own needles."

"Good, good," said the steward. He turned to Mrs Brown. "And you, dear lady?"

"I want to keep an eye on my husband," said Mrs Brown firmly.

Paddington found it hard to see what was going on when he joined the crowd at the start of the race, but he pricked up his ears when he heard Mrs Brown say she was worried Mr Brown might fall off his bicycle.

"He's going ever so slowly," agreed Judy.

"Leave it to me, everybody!" called Paddington. And he ran on to the track as fast as he could.

"Don't worry, Dad," called Jonathan from a nearby tent. "Wait until you see Mrs Bird's knitting. She's on a winning streak."

"Look at her needles," agreed Judy. "They're going like windmills. I hope she doesn't do herself a mischief."

"I expect she could do with a marmalade sandwich," said Paddington. "I brought some specially."

"Don't stop, Mrs Bird," he called. "I'm coming!"

The Browns' housekeeper had her hands full, so he popped a sandwich into her open mouth.

Mrs Bird gave a gurgle, but she didn't slow down.

"That's torn it," said Judy. "If Mrs Bird gets marmalade over her needles she won't be pleased."

"It's probably against the rules to feed competitors," said Mr Brown.

Jonathan gave a groan. "What's Paddington up to now?" he said.

"I've found some more wool if you run out, Mrs Bird," called Paddington.

"Grrr! Grrr!" spluttered Mrs Bird, shaking her head violently. "Grrr! Grrr!"

Paddington set to work. He had his back to Mrs Bird, so he didn't notice that as he wound the wool into a ball her piece of knitting grew smaller and smaller.

"Grrrrr!" said Mrs Bird. "Grrrrrrr! Grrrrrrrrrrr!"

"How on earth did he manage to do that?" asked Mr Brown.

"Don't even ask, Henry," replied Mrs Brown.

"Bang goes our last chance of a prize!" groaned Judy.

"We can't give up now," said Jonathan. "They're getting ready for the relay race. Who's for making up a foursome?"

Paddington's paw shot up. Judy raised her hand, and after a moment Mr Brown joined them.

"In for a penny, in for a pound," he said.

Judy made the first circuit of the track…

before passing the baton to Jonathan…

who in turn passed it to Paddington…

"Whatever you do," he gasped, "don't drop it."

Mr Brown was ready and waiting as a familiar figure rounded the bend.

"Where is it?" he cried, as Paddington drew alongside him. "The baton… where is it?"

"I don't know, Mr Brown," gasped Paddington. "I had it when
I left."

"You had it when you left?" repeated Mr Brown. "What do
you mean… you had it when you left?"

Paddington did his best to think of another way of saying
it. "Jonathan told me not to drop it…" he said. "So I put it
somewhere for safe keeping."

"I don't believe it," groaned Mr Brown.

As the race came to an end everybody cheered and began waving their hats in the air, so Paddington joined in.

"There it is!" cried Mrs Brown, pointing at Paddington's head. "It was under his hat all the time."

"I remember now," said Paddington.

"Don't be cross, Henry," said Mrs Brown. "It isn't as though he dropped it."

"Cross?" repeated Mr Brown. "Have you seen it? I'm thankful he *didn't* give it to me. It's covered in marmalade. Ugh! I think it's time we went home."

As the Browns were leaving, a man on the gate handed Paddington an envelope. "It's a small 'thank you'," he said. "You are our very first bear contestant and you seem to have brought us luck. Visitors have been flooding in."

The envelope contained a medal made of gold foil, and it had a ribbon attached so that Paddington could hang it round his neck. There was some writing across the front, but he was too excited to read it.

"I think," he announced, "I shall show it to Mr Curry. It might make his leg better."

"Mr Curry doesn't deserve it…" began Mrs Bird.

But Paddington was already on his way, and by the time they caught up with him all they heard was a cry of "Bear!", followed by a loud bang.

"Whatever happened?" asked Judy, as Paddington reappeared.

"Well," said Paddington, "when I showed Mr Curry my medal he started hopping about on one leg, but it was the wrong one, and when I mentioned it he slammed the door in my face."

"It's a pity you didn't mention the words on the front of the medal," said Mr Brown. "*Winning isn't everything. Taking part and doing your best is what matters most.*"

"I would rather someone else did that," said Paddington politely. "I don't think Mr Curry likes my mentions."

"After you, Henry," said Mrs Brown amid laughter all round.